Android Mae and Other Stories

Paula Luther

Published by Paula Luther, 2023.

ANDROID MAE AND OTHER STORIES

First edition. July 11, 2023.

ISBN: 979-8227264329

Written by Paula Luther.

Also by Paula Luther

Bart the Bard
Bart the Bard
The Bard and the Sorceress
The Bard and the Dragon
The Bard and the Siren

Standalone
The Queen of Fire
Android Mae and Other Stories

Table of Contents

Author's Note

This collection is born out of a love of science fiction and fantasy. Authors like Isaac Asimov, Robert A. Heinlein, J. R. R. Tolkien, and Brian Jacques inspired me to write stories of my own. Most of my teenage years were spent trying to become the next Great American Science Fiction Writer. Alas, that is a dream I do not think I will ever entirely fulfill. But some of the stories I wrote back then still held up when I re-read them as an adult, so I decided to go ahead and publish them.

To me, science fiction and fantasy are the whole reason that writing exists; they incorporate everything that draws us to stories in the first place. They are the pinnacle of imagination. Moreover, they serve as an effective way to explore and answer questions we may have about ourselves or the world in which we live. No other genres quite capture the freedom of limitless exploration the way that these two do. I daresay (though others will undoubtedly disagree with me) that they are the most important literary genres because they envelope the one quality that defines the human experience—curiosity and a quest for greater knowledge.

Android Mae

"Hi, Lance. Thanks for meeting me on such short notice," Jessi Grover greeted her fiancé.

Lance March rose from his outdoor table at the restaurant. "No problem, Jessi. Have you eaten yet?"

"Yeah, I grabbed an apple on my way here," Jessi shrugged as she slid into the facing chair.

"I mean a real meal."

"Haven't eaten anything since breakfast; been too busy." She eyed his leftover meatloaf sandwich. "Are you going to eat that?"

Lance wordlessly pushed the plate toward Jessi, who grabbed the sandwich and shoved it into her mouth. Her eyes closed in ecstasy. "Lance March, you are the most wonderful man in the world." She pulled out some papers from a bag and spread them out over the table. "Now, about the table arrangement..."

She rambled on and on about assorted plans for their wedding, but Lance didn't seem to be listening. Finally Jessi snorted, "Lance, are you even listening to me?"

"What?" Lance snapped out of his trance. "Sorry, Jess. I was thinking."

"So I noticed. About what?"

"Remember how my sister-in-law died from cancer last year?" Lance asked.

"How could I forget Mae?" Jessi replied. "She was my best friend; she introduced us."

"Remember how rough it was on Ed?" Lance continued.

"Do I ever," Jessi shook her head. "He wouldn't leave his house for weeks."

"Things have taken a turn for the worse again," Lance admitted.

"What happened?" Jessi questioned anxiously.

"About two months ago he started showing up late to various things—his job, church, stuff like that. I tried to talk to him, but he shooed me out of his house and hasn't answered any of my calls. Then today I got a call from his boss. It seems Ed hasn't shown up at work in three weeks."

"Maybe he quit," Jessi suggested.

"He never handed in any notices or gave any indication that he planned on quitting," Lance refuted. "As far as their records show, he's still employed there. I was going to try to see him after lunch today."

"I'll come, too," Jessi decided.

"Jess, this is my problem, not yours," Lance argued.

"But Ed will be my brother in three months," Jessi countered. "This is my problem, too." She rose and gathered her papers, stuffing them back in her bag. "Are you coming or not?"

"I'm right behind you," Lance surrendered.

DR. EDWIN MARCH HUNCHED over the kitchen table where he had his work spread all over the place. Being one of the most talented roboticists that ever walked the face of the earth had its advantages. Let everyone see if *he* would stand by and let cancer rob him of his wife!

He ran his hand maniacally through his thick, silver-flecked black hair as he muttered to himself, "Circuit A to connect to port C; let E feed to N..."

This, his piece de resistance, his magnum opus, was almost finished when he heard the doorbell ring. "Go away!" he shouted.

"Ed! Ed, it's Lance and Jessi. Let us in!" his brother's voice called.

"No! Leave me alone!"

"Ed, please," Jessi pleaded.

"Go away!" Ed repeated. "Don't bother me!"

"If you don't open this door in five seconds, I'm forcing my way in," Lance threatened.

That got Ed's attention. He straightened, shoved his glasses back up his face, and opened the door, glowering at the people on the doorstep. "What do you want? I'm very busy."

"We wanted to see if you were alive," Lance responded with a hint of anger.

"Won't you let us in?" Jessi queried.

"No," Ed refused grumpily. "You've seen I'm alive; now go." He began to close the door, but Lance caught it and forced it open.

"Not so fast, big brother. I've got some questions, and I want answers." Lance entered and motioned for Jessi to follow.

"What are those questions?" Ed wanted to know.

"Your boss called me today. You haven't been at work in three weeks. They hadn't heard anything from you–no calls, no e-mails, nothing. And speaking of calls, you haven't answered mine for the past two months. What's going on?" Lance demanded.

Ed opened his mouth to reply but closed it again and appeared to be thinking. Finally he said, "I had hoped to keep this a secret, but it is close enough to being ready that I suppose I can tell you. I know I can trust you two."

"Trust us with what?" Jessi ventured.

"Follow me," Ed beckoned.

Lance and Jessi exchanged dubious glances and followed Ed into the kitchen. There they saw what appeared to be a woman lying face-down on the table. Ed turned her over and eased her to a sitting position. Her black hair flowed down freely over her shoulders, but her brown eyes showed no expression whatsoever.

"Is that..." Jessi gasped. "It can't be."

"It isn't," Lance answered grimly. "But I can guess at what it is." He turned accusingly to Ed. "You built a robot replica of Mae."

"Android, not robot," Ed corrected.

"Same difference," Lance shrugged.

"Not at all," Ed told him. "Androids are humanoid robots, and that is exactly what this is. And a very sophisticated model, too; I doubt if there's ever been anything like it." He couldn't keep a note of pride out of his voice. "I programmed it to have facial expressions, emotions, and all of Mae's characteristics."

"And this is the reason you haven't been at work?" Lance asked.

"Yes," Ed confessed. "It didn't start out that way. I've been working on this for almost a full year. Actually, I started only a few weeks after Mae died. I worked on it a little here and there.

As I got closer to completion, it seemed to possess me. I *had* to finish. I had to have my wife again."

"But it's not your wife," Jessi whispered. "It'll never be your wife. It's just a–a thing. It's not even human, not even alive."

"Who are you to say what this is and is not?" Ed thundered. "Were you here when I programmed it to smile as she did? Were you here when I covered it with skin and hair to give it her appearance? Were you here when I gave it eyes that mirror hers?"

Jessi backed away, trembling. "Ed," she breathed.

"Don't say anything, Jessi," Lance cautioned.

"She will live! She will return to me!" Ed exalted.

"Lance," Jessi murmured anxiously, sending him a worried glance.

His mini-monologue completed, Ed turned back to the android and pressed a depression on the back of its neck. The eyes blinked, and the head turned to Ed.

"Do you know who you are?" Ed questioned.

"I am Mae March," it responded. "You are Edwin March. I am your wife." Indicating Lance and Jessi: "Who are they?"

"This is my brother Lance March, and this is his fiancée, Jessi Grover. Jessi is your best friend, and you introduced them to each other," Ed explained.

"I have no memory of either of them," android Mae stated.

"You won't," Ed told it. "You have...a memory problem. I will supply you with all information you need."

The android nodded stiffly and hoisted itself off the table. It walked stiffly into the kitchen.

"Where are you going?" Ed asked.

"We have guests. I must prepare food."

"We've already eaten," Lance excused.

"That is irrelevant." The android continued on its way.

Ed beamed at them proudly. "What do you think?" he wanted to know.

"From a mechanical point of view it's most impressive," Lance agreed. "But there's no way in a thousand years anyone will think for a minute that's Mae!"

"I know there are still some bugs to work out," Ed admitted sheepishly, rubbing the back of his neck. "But I've never tried anything like this before. I think it turned out pretty well, don't you?"

Jessi stared numbly. "Lance, I think I'm ready to go home now," she ventured.

"You can at least stay for a sandwich, can't you?" Ed begged. "I programmed the android with Mae's phenomenal culinary skills."

"I'm hearing a lot of 'I programmed it to do blah-blah-blah,'" Lance commented. "Doesn't that bother you? You didn't have to program the real Mae."

"Nothing is too big a challenge if it means having my wife back," Ed assured him.

Lance sighed and glanced at Jessi. "Well, I hope you're still hungry. Looks like we've been invited to stay."

"I think I lost my appetite," Jessi confessed.

"Jessi, don't you see how wonderful this is?" Ed asked in amazement. "I have created a near-perfect replica of my dead wife—your best friend! You should be filled with joy at seeing her alive again!"

"She's not alive again!" Jessi exploded. "I don't care what you say; that's not Mae! Lance, I'm sorry, but I really want to be heading home now."

"Can't say I blame you," Lance agreed, sending a meaningful look in Ed's direction. "Tell your android thanks but no thanks. Come on, Jessi."

They left the house without looking back.

"They'll come around," Ed muttered.

At the moment Lance and Jessi didn't particularly feel like coming around. They drove wordlessly to Jessi's apartment, not speaking. Right as Lance pulled up, Jessi broke the silence.

"Was he serious?"

"As serious as I've ever seen him," Lance admitted.

"Something's wrong, Lance. I think he snapped."

"I think you're right."

"What are you going to do?"

"I don't know. I can't throw him in an asylum; that's for certain."

"Why not? He's obviously sick."

"For one thing, Jessi, Ed would have to agree to be institutionalized, and he'd never do that. For another, he's my brother. I couldn't do it."

"But if it's for his own good–"

"I won't do it." The finality in his voice was unmistakable. "Right now I think all I can do is keep an eye on him. If things get really bad, I'll make my move then."

"How will you define things as really bad?" Jessi wanted to know.

"I'll know when I see it," Lance assured. "Trust me."

Jessi sighed and shook her head. "I really think you should do something now before things get worse," she advised.

"He's my brother. I think I can handle this," Lance snapped. "I believe this is your stop, Miss Grover."

"Indeed it is, Mr. March." Without so much as a goodbye or a "Don't call me; I'll call you," Jessi got out of the car and slammed the door quite ferociously, stalking up to the door and slamming that, too.

Lance pounded his steering wheel in frustration. Why did things have to take such a sudden nasty turn with Jessi? They hadn't had an argument on this magnitude for ages, not since that stupid little disagreement about whether or not he could keep his ancient pit bull once they were married (Jessi relented and said Dusty could stick around till he died of old age, which, judging from how he kept recovering from near-death experiences, might be sometime next century).

I hope this doesn't ruin our wedding, he thought. *But if it does, then maybe it's a sign we shouldn't be married.*

"HOW WAS YOUR SUPPER?" android Mae inquired as anxiously as it could. As the day progressed, it had begun to act less android and more human.

"Most excellent," Ed smiled, wiping his mouth with a napkin. "You've outdone yourself, Mae."

"Thank you," android Mae returned. It smiled as the real Mae often had, but its eyes were cold and empty, without life or spark. It was little better than an animated corpse, but Ed overlooked this and watched as it retreated into the kitchen to wash the dishes. He went into the living room to watch the news.

About ten minutes later android Mae entered the living room and sat down in what had been the real Mae's favorite chair, a plush, deep green rocker-recliner. It reached into a yarn basket positioned on the left and brought up a scarf Mae had been crocheting before she died. It curled up exactly the way Mae used to and began to crochet.

Ed had programmed the android with as many of Mae's characteristics as he could, but it still surprised and slightly disquieted him to see a replicate machine so perfectly duplicating his wife's actions.

I'm starting to think like Lance and Jessi, he scolded himself. *They must have rubbed off on me. Just ignore them. You knew this would take some getting used to.* "How are you doing with the scarf?"

"I'm not sure," android Mae frowned, holding up the yarn. "I don't remember starting this scarf."

"I said you had some problems with your memory," Ed reminded quietly.

"Have I always?" android Mae wanted to know.

"N–no," Ed choked. Those eyes! Those lifeless, staring eyes! "It started–" He broke off.

"Edwin?"

Ed blinked away the tears. "I'm sorry, Mae. It–was very difficult for me to watch you go through– the ordeal that caused you to lose your memory."

"Will I ever have my memories back?"

"No. I'm sorry."

For an instant the android almost looked sad, but Ed reminded himself that this was a result of the artificial emotions he programmed into it. "What if I see someone I'm supposed to know and don't recognize them?"

"I'll help you," Ed promised. "Wait a minute." He went to one of the shelves and got a photo album. He crossed back to the android and opened the album. "These are some of your pictures. They'll help you remember people and places in your background."

It opened to the first page and jabbed at a picture of two black-haired girls sitting in a rubber pool. "Who are they?"

"That's a picture of you and your sister Elly," Ed explained. "Elly lives in Cleveland now; she's a reporter for the local newspaper."

Android Mae seemed to accept this explanation without question and calmly turned the page. For each picture of family and friends Ed was there to provide an identity. It learned very rapidly and was even able to recognize Jessi in an old high-school picture.

At last it came to the most important pictures of all. "What event do these pictures represent?"

"They represent my—our—wedding day," Ed replied.

"Wedding day? I do not understand," android Mae admitted.

"It's the day we were married," Ed expanded.

Android Mae nodded understandingly and peered more closely at the pictures. "I would think that I would remember such an important day," it mused. "You are not angry with me that I forgot, are you?"

"No," Ed reassured. "The memory loss wasn't your fault. I know you'd remember if you could."

"I shall try to remember," it promised.

"Thank you." Ed choked on the words. It would try so hard to be Mae, but it just wouldn't succeed.

IT WAS THE MORNING after the argument, and Lance found a message on his answering machine. The caller ID revealed Jessi's name. He almost deleted the message but thought better of it. He hit the play button and sat down to finish his oatmeal.

"Hey, Lance, it's me. Um, I'm sorry about what happened yesterday. It wasn't my place to dictate what you should or shouldn't do about your brother. Are you there? Are you going to return my call?" The message ended there.

Lance contemplated Jessi's message while eating his oatmeal with one hand and rubbing Dusty's head with the other. Should he return her call or not? She was right; she had no business telling him what to do about Ed now that he'd turned into Dr. Frankenstein. Ed was his problem, not hers. Maybe it would be better to meet in person and discuss everything.

Picking up the phone, he dialed her number. Not surprisingly, he got her voice mail. "Hi, Jessi, it's Lance. How about meeting at the cafe for lunch this afternoon? I think we need to talk. You can get back to me with a good time for you. I love you."

The ball's in your court now, Jess, he thought as he hung up.

IT WAS A VERY MEEK Jessi that met Lance that afternoon. She studiously avoided looking at him as he sat down.

"Aren't you going to order lunch?" Lance asked.

"I already ate," Jessi murmured, writing something in her plan book. Once she finished, she looked up at her fiancé. "Is this where I apologize?"

Lance nodded wordlessly.

"All right." She inhaled deeply. "I'm sorry, Lance. It wasn't right of me to disagree with you over how to handle Ed. He's not my brother...yet."

"And I'm sorry I lost my temper," Lance apologized. "I shouldn't have snapped. Friends?"

Jessi gave the enchanting smile that made Lance fall in love with her in the first place. "I always thought we were more than friends."

"We were–are–but this doesn't mean I don't want your advice," Lance told her. "In fact, I'd welcome it wholeheartedly."

"You have it," Jessi promised. "And in a few more months you'll have unlimited access to my horde of advice for the rest of your life."

"Hip hip hooray," Lance grinned.

"You'd better be enthusiastic," Jessi mock scolded. "Seriously, though, what are we going to do about Ed?"

"The only thing we can do right now is wait and see what happens," Ed shrugged. "I wish there was something more, but there isn't."

Jessi nodded in agreement. "All right. We'll wait."

There was silence for a few minutes before Lance asked, "Is that it? Aren't there any wedding details you need to discuss with me?"

Jessi pulled out her ubiquitous notebook (Lance began to wonder if it was attached to her in some way) and flipped several pages before finding the one she wanted. "Well, my cousins and I were trying to organize the flower arrangements, but we can't get it quite right. I don't think you'll find it very interesting, though."

"Let me see," Lance invited. "It's my wedding, too, you know." He studied the page Jessi showed him. At first it seemed like nothing more than gibberish, but gradually a pattern appeared. "Well, why don't you move the roses over here and the lilies right"—he squinted for a moment—"here?" He indicated the new positions.

Jessi took back her notebook, studied the changes, and hugged Lance across the table. "Lance, you're a genius, a bona-fide genius, and I'm so glad I'm marrying you!"

"Jessi, you're choking me," Lance gasped.

"Sorry." Jessi released him and returned to her seat. "This makes everything a whole lot clearer. Thanks again."

"No problem," Lance smiled.

"Now I have to be going. My lunch break's almost over. See you later."

"Bye, Jessi."

TIME PROGRESSED, AND Lance and Jessi continued the happy preparations for their wedding. It would have been perfect if they still weren't worried about Edwin. He had returned to work and other aspects of his social life, and he had begun bringing android Mae to family gatherings and parties. He garnered a few strange looks, but nobody questioned him. What was especially frightening to Lance and Jessi, however, was his complete acceptance of the machine. He acted as if it really and truly was Mae.

"I'm scared for him, Lance," Jessi remarked at their rehearsal banquet. Edwin and android Mae weren't there, so talking about the situation was safe. "His mind's sort of shut off."

"You think you're scared? Only last week he was scolding me for being so cold to 'Mae'! 'You used to like her,' he said. Jessi, this is beginning to feel like something out of a horror novel."

"What do we do?"

"There's nothing we can do right now. Besides, if we tried an intervention or something like that, his mind might snap. No, it seems we can only wait and pray."

"We've been waiting and praying for the last three months."

"Then we just need to keep it up."

AS JESSI PUT THE FINISHING touches on her makeup the morning of her wedding, her phone trilled sharply. Sighing, she reached for her cell only to see Lance's number in the caller ID.

"I thought the groom wasn't supposed to see the bride before the wedding," she reminded him in greeting.

"There's no convention against phone calls. Jess, we've got a problem."

"What's up?"

"Ed's not here. I saw him last night, and he promised to come early. But he's not here; he won't even answer his phone. I must have sent a dozen texts—"

"Ed knows how to text?" Jessi interrupted in surprise.

"Of course," Lance answered.

"He just didn't strike me as the texting type," Jessi shrugged.

"He doesn't like it, but he knows how to do it," Lance explained. "What if he did something drastic?"

"How drastic are we talking?" Jessi wanted to know.

"Drastic like running off with android Mae—or maybe something worse. Jessi, I'm scared," he admitted.

"Calm down, Lance," she soothed. "Why don't you go check on him?"

"But we're getting married in a half hour."

"I'm not going anywhere. Of course, the hungry masses will be ticked because it'll delay the reception."

"No, Jessi." Lance was firm. "Our lives have been revolving around my insane brother for the last three months; today is about us—you and me and the life we're beginning together. He could just be cranky because he knows we don't want Mae here."

"All right," Jessi agreed hesitantly.

"We can stop in after the wedding and see how he's doing then," Lance added.

"Sure." She glanced at the clock. "I have to go now, Lance. See you soon."

"Love you, Jess."

Jessi closed her phone and steadied her breathing. She was excited to be marrying Lance, yet she knew her thoughts would revolve around Ed all day.

I hope he's all right.

WHEN ED WOKE THAT MORNING, he had every intention of attending Lance and Jessi's wedding. He raided his closet and dug out his old tuxedo, confident that it still fit.

Android Mae observed him calmly as he examined his appearance in the mirror. "You look very sharp, Ed. Where are you going?"

Ever since he had adjusted the android's dialogue malfunctions, it had become much easier to think of his creation as the real Mae. "Lance and Jessi are getting married today."

"What?" Android Mae rose from her seat on the edge of the bed in shock. "Why wasn't I told?"

As Ed searched for a reason, android Mae continued, "Jessi's my best friend! Things haven't exactly been easy between us the last three months, but she's still my friend. And you're my husband; what were you thinking hiding something this big from me!?"

"They didn't want you there," Ed blurted out before he realized the implications of his admittance.

"THEY DIDN'T WANT ME there!? What have I done that they don't want me at their wedding? Is it related to my memory loss?" Its eyes widened in horror. "Did I do something really bad that got them mad at me?"

"They're not mad at you, Mae," he assured it. "If they're mad at anyone, it's me." He sank dejectedly onto the bed.

"If they're mad at you, why are they taking it out on me?" android Mae inquired gently as it sat next to Ed. "They stare at me with such poorly-disguised disgust. Why, Ed?"

"I can't answer that," he whispered.

"Yes, you can" it insisted. "You know why they don't like me. Tell me."

"I can't."

"Ed! What is it; why do they hate me!?"

"Because you're an android!" Ed screamed.

Oh, now I've done it, he thought disgustedly. He had never known how his android would react if it learned it was a machine, but he was about to find out. "The real Mae March died from cancer over a year ago. I made you out of my grief to replace her, to bring her back to life." His voice broke. "I couldn't live without her."

It shook its head fiercely. "You're wrong. I *am* Mae! You told me I was!"

"Told you, yes! You didn't know it on your own. That should tell you something."

"It tells me I had amnesia! What sort of sick joke is this?" Its eyes began to burn. "I

don't know what you're trying to do, but I'm going to Lance and Jessi's wedding with you." With that, it stalked to the closet and began examining the dresses.

"Listen to me!" Ed grabbed it by the shoulders and tried to turn it around. The android resisted, pushing him to the ground. Desperately he raised himself and grabbed its arm, trying to pull it away from the closet, but android Mae refused to be moved. In the midst of the ensuing scuffle, Ed inadvertently slammed the android against the wall. A sharp crack split the air, and the automaton went limp in his arms.

What have I done? Ed thought in horror. Frantically he examined the damage, but his vision was blurring too badly to see properly.

Within what seemed a few minutes, Ed found himself sitting up slowly on his couch with no memory of how he had gotten there.

"Ed, you're awake!" a voice gasped in relief.

He turned to see Jessi approaching him with a cup of water in her hands.

As he pushed himself up, he saw in horror that the fall had cracked the android's head. The expression on its face was frozen in shock and rage; its very presence caused something in Ed to snap. He screamed and starting tearing the carpet frenziedly.

No! Not again! I can't lose her again! I won't *lose her again!* He examined the crack, hoping there was some way he could fix it.

Ed struck the wall quite hard and blacked out for a few seconds. As he started to revive, he noticed he was laying in a hospital bed with all sorts of machines attached to him. His eyes flicked around the room, eventually settling on a woman sitting in a nearby chair. Her head was lowered as she dozed in the chair.

Did it bring me here? he wondered. Hesitantly he called softly, "Mae?"

The woman raised her head, and Ed's breath stuck in his throat. This wasn't the android! It was Mae! But how?

"Ed, you're awake!" she breathed in relief, rushing over to grab his hand. "We were so worried."

"You're alive," he croaked around the breathing tube in his throat. "Or I'm dead."

"Well, I'm certainly not dead," Mae teased gently, "so you're definitely alive."

"No," Ed shook his head. He propped himself up carefully, wondering why he felt so sore. He had only bashed his head when he fell; why did his entire body hurt? "You're dead. You died last year from cancer. I was there."

She frowned, puzzled. "Ed, you've been in a coma for the last nine days. Don't you remember the bus?"

"The bus?" His mind began to clear, and pieces of his memory started returning. He remembered crossing the street as he walked to work. He had been in a hurry, hadn't looked before he stepped off the sidewalk..."And I've been in a coma for nine days?"

"Yes," Mae nodded. "Lance, Jessi, and I have been taking turns sitting here waiting for you to wake up. You know, I think Lance and Jessi would make a nice couple. I'll have to tell Lance to ask her out."

"So none of it happened," Ed murmured.

"None of what happened?" Mae wanted to know.

"Nothing. It was just a crazy dream I had."

Mae gave a small nod and told him, "I'll go tell the nurse you're awake." She squeezed his hand again. "I'm so glad you're awake."

"So am I," Ed agreed.

End

The Sasquatch Search

Author's Note: "The Sasquatch Search" is told from the viewpoint of Ashley Mackee, one of my oldest recurring characters in my stories. She first appeared in "Show Time" in 2006 as part of my entry in a youth short story competition. Although her stories were originally intended to be generic tales of a girl and her horse, I couldn't resist the idea of putting a science fiction twist on one of her adventures.

My most recent adventure began on an ordinary afternoon. The weather was brisk but not chill; the sky was clear and blue, and I was riding Zorro, my four-year-old black Arabian stallion, on my way to the library. The family's books were due, and I volunteered to return them. I had been looking for an excuse to ride Zorro, anyway; the weather was too perfect to waste.

I chose to take a shortcut through the woods, which contained a little-used trail that served as a back way to town. It was one of the best places to ride although Zorro didn't use to think so. When I first adopted Zorro from a horse rescue shelter, riding him could be unpredictable. He spooked easily and was very suspicious of anything he didn't understand. Now, however, he walked the wooded trail with perfect poise; the only indication that he heard the usual forest noises was the occasional swish of his ears. The forest itself seemed unusually calm, and I had trouble concentrating on where to leave the path and head for the main road. Just as I did find the junction, Zorro dug all four legs into the ground and refused to move.

"What's wrong?" I asked in disgust, wondering why he suddenly balked. "I don't hear anything."

His nostrils flared, and he rose into a semi-rear. I managed to get him down, but now he was jogging in place and snorting like crazy; I could see the whites of his eyes.

Then I heard a strange sound, like a series of loud grunts—*very* loud grunts. Something crashed through the woods off to my right. As I turned to get a better glimpse, Zorro screamed and went up in a full rear, forelegs thrashing as though he were trying to fight an enemy.

Now I was frightened. Zorro had spooked in these woods before, but he had never reacted like this to a bush, rabbit, or squirrel. I struggled to get him back down, speaking soothingly and rubbing his coat in all his favorite places. When he finally calmed somewhat, I looked back to where I had heard the crashing noises. The tall, majestic trees were twisted and bent in unnatural positions, and a path was now present where there hadn't been a path before. Curiosity overcame fear, and I nudged Zorro forward. He refused to move.

"You know, I once read somewhere that Arabians are the only horses brave enough to face lions," I remarked, fostering a silly little hope of shaming him into moving. I didn't know if Zorro had understood me, but my comment didn't work; his hooves remained firmly entrenched in the ground. After much coaxing, he approached the new path hesitantly. His nostrils flared once more, and I could see the whites of his eyes again. He was ready to bolt if the whatever-it-was returned. Leaning over his shoulder, I examined the ground. A trail of giant footprints led into the overgrown shrubs. I had seen footprints like that on TV specials and the internet. I had never expected to see them so close to home.

My heart hammering, I wheeled Zorro around. "Let's get to the library."

THE REST OF OUR TRIP was uneventful. Zorro took a few minutes to calm down before we were able to continue to the library. He was still snorting suspiciously and tossing his head as I dropped his reins to the ground and ordered, "Stay."

He shifted uneasily for a few seconds before settling down. Those ground-tying lessons had come in handy yet again. After returning the books and chatting briefly with the librarian, I took Zorro home on the main road. My initial explanation was that I didn't want Zorro to spook again, but I later had to admit that I was afraid, too. The afternoon's encounter had all the earmarks of a Bigfoot sighting, from the loud grunting to the smashed trees to the giant footprints, and I didn't know what to do. After all, how often is it that someone has to deal with an urban legend practically in one's backyard?

What do I do if it is a Sasquatch? I wondered as I turned Zorro into the driveway, for I didn't know what else it could be. I noticed the blue Volkswagen beetle that belonged to Abby, my twenty-one-year-old art student sister, was back, so I assumed she'd made it home for dinner. Considering how long some of her past student meetings had run, I was surprised she was back this early. Continuing into the backyard, I was even more surprised to see Dave and Chrissy, my eighteen-year-old brother and twelve-year-old sister, leaning against Zorro's barn.

Gladiator, our chocolate Labrador Retriever, snoozed in the grass.

"What are you doing out here?" I questioned, dismounting and leading Zorro to his barn.

"Abby's got a crisis," Dave grimaced.

"How bad?" I wanted to know.

"Very," Chrissy assured me. "I wouldn't be out here otherwise."

I nodded understandingly while I put Zorro in the crossties to keep him still. Gladiator, noticing our arrival, trotted over to Zorro and sniffed his leg. Zorro sniffed back.

"Why'd you come home the main way?" Dave queried casually.

As I hung the bridle back on its peg and unbuckled the saddle, I thought of a way to explain to my siblings what happened. Somehow I was reluctant to talk about it, and I didn't know why. Eventually I replied, "Something spooked Zorro in the woods this afternoon, and I didn't want it to happen again." Deftly I changed the subject. "So what's the nature of Abby's latest crisis?"

"Apparently the students in her study group had a big misunderstanding about something," Dave shrugged. "I'm not sure I understand all the details."

"It was quite dramatic," Chrissy added. "Now Abby's saying there's no chance they can ever be friends again."

"Is she saying all of this in a lofty tone?" I checked.

"Oh, yes," Chrissy confirmed. "She's even started drawing parallels with Jane Austen novels."

"Yikes." The three of us were ready to stay outside until Abby's sanity returned, but it was too close to suppertime.

Instead, we squared our shoulders and prepared ourselves for a very long evening of listening to our eldest sibling's woes.

A long evening it was. Even Chrissy, Abby's staunchest supporter, couldn't stand the drama and sought refuge in the basement with Dave and me. We played some video games and watched a movie we could actually agree on (a remarkable feat that can only happen once every three years with a full moon and planetary alignment). The three of us had a fun time while Tropical Storm Abby raged upstairs, yet I couldn't stop thinking about the creature Zorro and I had encountered in the woods. Was it a Sasquatch? Was it dangerous? What—if anything—could I do about it? These questions tumbled inside my head all night and most of the next morning. The incessant nagging finally drove me to take my small digital/video camera into the woods early next afternoon, traveling on Zorro to get back to the part of the woods where he had spooked. He didn't spook this time, but he was wary.

I dismounted, tied his reins to a tree branch, and approached the trail of giant footprints. Taking out my camera, I began photographing the marks.

"Hi, Ashley!" a familiar voice called in greeting.

I turned and waved at my best friend Maureen Turf, who was trotting towards me on her eleven-year-old chestnut Morgan gelding Coffee. Zorro whinnied in greeting they approached.

"I was just on my way to visit you; what are you doing here?" she asked cheerfully.

"Something so crazy I can barely believe I'm doing it," I shook my head.

"Which is..." Maureen prompted.

I glanced around. No one else seemed to be here, and I knew I could trust Maureen to keep a secret like this. "Yesterday Zorro and I were on our way to the library when something crashed through these woods."

Maureen leaned over to get a better look. "Yeah, I thought this path looked clearer than before. It must have been big."

"It was," I affirmed, "and it spooked Zorro like nothing else. And look at these footprints."

She dismounted, tied Coffee to a nearby tree, and knelt by one of the footprints. Her fine black eyebrows shot up her forehead. "Whoa," she breathed.

"Yeah. Whoa," I agreed.

"Are you going to follow the trail?"

"I'm going to try."

"Can I help?"

"Of course," I grinned, happy that my best friend was willing to help me one what might prove to be the stupidest thing I'd ever do. "Riders up."

We mounted our horses and set off down the trail. As Zorro and Coffee ambled along, I switched my camera to video mode to film footage for a documentary.

"This is a possible trail of the elusive Sasquatch, known better as Bigfoot, and we, Jennifer and Agnes, are following to see what lies at the end," I reported in my best investigative journalist voice, which quavered from nervousness just a little bit. I decided to use Maureen's and my middle names because, in the conspiracy-theory thoughts swirling through my brain at the time, it might provide protection from shadowy underworld characters that might target us for uncovering such mind-blowing knowledge.

The situation's intense edge diminished somewhat when an off-camera Maureen complained, "Why do I have to be Agnes? I hate that name; why can't you be Agnes?"

Sighing, I paused the recording and retorted, "Agnes isn't my middle name. Besides, do you think I like Jennifer?"

"Fine, fine," Maureen grumbled.

That disagreement settled, I resumed recording and went on for some time about the history of Bigfoot sightings, knowledge I hadn't realized I had amassed but must have gleaned from too many late-night documentaries. Eventually I shut off the camera to save the batteries.

The sun began to sink, and we hadn't found anything. I began to wonder if we would have to call off the search.

"We should probably turn back," Maureen suggested. "I told my mom I'd help make supper, and Coffee doesn't gallop the way he used to."

"But"—I protested.

"But nothing, Ashley. I really do have to be going."

"You're right," I agreed. "We can continue this another day."

One day turned into another and into yet another, and we still didn't find anything. Some days Maureen investigated with me, but more frequently I was alone. The idea that I might find a Sasquatch living in our very own woods practically monopolized all my time; it was all I ever thought about.

"What are you going to do if you do find it?" Maureen wondered one day as she joined me on my search. By now I had ventured farther into the woods than I had ever gone before, and I just knew I'd find something.

"I don't know," I shrugged. "Revel in the knowledge I found Bigfoot, I suppose."

"Is that all?" she pressed.

"As of right now, yes. Am I supposed to have a bigger plan?"

Her clear blue eyes clouded thoughtfully. "I just thought it was strange that you've spent so much time searching for Bigfoot and haven't thought of what you were going to do afterwards."

As I considered my reply, I heard the same grunt that had echoed through the woods that fateful afternoon. Zorro began to snort nervously, and the normally sleepy Coffee perked up a bit.

"We should probably leave the horses here," I whispered.

Maureen nodded silently, and we both slid off our mounts and tied them to branches. Zorro calmed slightly when he got the chance to "talk" with Coffee. Satisfied they would be all right, Maureen and I crept towards the sound. I got out my camera and recorded everything. I was talking a bit faster than usual due to nervousness.

"After many weeks of searching, Agnes and I have found the end of the trail. We can hear the same noise that accompanied the creature's presence in the forest the first time...and I think I'm hearing more than one."

Maureen had gone a bit further than I had and had reached a small clearing by some shrubs. I could see her gesturing emphatically for me to hurry up. When I finally joined her, my jaw dropped as I observed a real, live Sasquatch entering the clearing from the other side of the forest. Judging from the clumps of berries gathered in its huge, muscular arms, it had been foraging. It paused in its walk and emitted a long, low wail. Almost immediately its cry was answered threefold, two of which sounded rather high-pitched. Maureen and I gaped as another Sasquatch strode into view followed by two younger individuals that were nearly as tall as adult humans. All of them were covered with dark brown fur except for their palms and soles. We hadn't found just one Bigfoot—we had found an entire family! I recorded everything they did, elated that my search had finally paid off.

Maureen and I could have stayed for hours, but the camera's batteries were running low, and it beeped to tell me so. That's when the trouble started.

As I shut off the camera, Maureen clutched my arm. "Ashley!"

I looked up in time to see the parents starting for our hiding place.

"Let's get out of here!" I urged.

We scrambled up and dashed for the horses, very much aware that the parents were close behind. One of them let out a roar, and we ran all the faster. We barely reached the horses in time; the parents were intent on eliminating a threat to their children. Zorro and Coffee were anxious to get out of hearing and smelling range; they galloped faster than they ever had before. Eventually the roars died down, and we were alone once more.

"How long do you think they've been there?" Maureen wondered after several minutes.

"Difficult to say," I replied. "They're known to migrate—they could have been coming here all these years without anyone's seeing anything. That part of the woods is certainly thick enough to hide a whole herd of Sasquatches."

"So now what are you going to do?"

I hesitated several seconds before admitting, "I don't know. I considered taking the video to a news station or something, but

I have very slim chances of being believed. I really don't know, Maureen. I feel kind of lost now."

"That's what you get for not thinking things through," she mock-scolded. "You're like a sister to me, Ashley, but you do have a tendency to jump into situations head-first. That's how you got Zorro, remember?"

"And do you remember a certain friend who encouraged me, 'Get him, Ashley. You'll be fine.'?" I retorted.

Maureen grinned ruefully. "Yeah, I suppose I did do that. But that turned out all right, wouldn't you say?"

"Yeah, I guess it did." I mirrored her grin. "We've still got some daylight. Feel like riding by the creek?"

"Sure. I could use some normality after this." She squeezed Coffee's sides, urging him into a trot. Zorro matched his gait easily, and Maureen and I chatted about everything except Sasquatches. Thus ended another of the frankly zany adventures in which Zorro and I have found ourselves in the past. No doubt there would be more, but at least next time I was better prepared to properly think through any grand plans I might have.

End

Counterattack

Elaine woke up with a dizzying headache. Everything was blurry, and she didn't know where she was. To top everything off, she could barely move her legs. Slowly she pushed herself up with her arms and got a good look at her surroundings once her vision cleared. She seemed to be in a dark room with extremely dim lights flickering outside the door.

How did I get here? she wondered. Remembering anything, even her own name, proved to be an unpleasant chore, so she instead rubbed and slapped her legs until the feeling returned.

At first Elaine didn't notice anything strange, but then something struck her with as much force as a train. She wasn't wearing the outfit she remembered putting on that night. Instead she was wearing a loose brown dress, a dress she had never seen before in her life.

Where am I? she thought with increasing panic. Standing up, she approached the door to her room. It wasn't locked and swung open with the lightest touch; soon Elaine found herself in an equally dim hallway.

"Hello?" she called hesitantly. "Is anyone there?"

Footsteps clacked behind her, and she whipped around to face the newcomer, a slim young woman wearing a lab coat.

"I was beginning to wonder when you'd wake up," she remarked offhandedly, pulling a light cord as she passed it.

Elaine's breath caught in her throat and came out in a sickly choking sound. It was like looking in a mirror. The woman was physically identical to her! The high cheekbones, tiny snub nose, and large grey eyes were all too familiar to Elaine.

"Who are you?" she wheezed.

A harsh smile touched her double's lips, and Elaine then noticed a slight difference. Her eyes had always had a kind, cheerful light kindled inside, but this other woman's eyes were colder.

"I'm you, sort of," the stranger replied.

"What?"

"Allow me to introduce myself. I'm Marie Elaine Hart. *Dr.* Marie Elaine Hart. Does that name me anything to you?"

"That's my name in reverse," Elaine realized, "without the Dr. prefix, of course. But that still doesn't tell me who you are."

"When I said I was you, I meant I was your counterpart," Marie explained.

"You mean like a twin?" Elaine suggested.

"Partly. If it makes things easier, you can think of me as a twin." Marie shoved her hands in her pockets. "I know you don't know much about theoretical physics, but I'll explain everything as simply as I can. I am a version of you from a different timeline."

Elaine blinked blankly. "What?"

"Every choice every person makes is a flux-point where things could go either way. That branching created different realities for you and me. For example, I am a physicist for a top-secret government research facility, and I know you are a receptionist at a newspaper office. We made different choices about our careers."

"I remember that!" Elaine exclaimed. "I read an article in a magazine about theoretical physics and wanted to enter that field. But then I thought things through"—

"You thought too much work was involved," Marie snapped, "and you decided not to pursue that option. I didn't care about the work; that's what I wanted to do. And now I have a Ph.D., a well-paying job, and the most miserable life I can imagine."

"How can your life be miserable?" Elaine asked in amazement. "It sounds pretty good to me."

"That's because you don't live it," Marie responded bitterly. "It's a life full of politicking and back-stabbing, not to mention some of the uses to which our breakthroughs have been put. I hate it, I tell you. *I hate it*!"

"Okay, but how do I come into this?" Elaine wanted to know.

Marie's eyes burned brightly. "I'm the one who first made inter-reality jumps possible. Once I made it happen, I realized this was my chance to change my life. I could become someone else and finally be free. It was at least worth a try. So I extracted you from your timeline with the intention of replacing you."

"You mean you'll be living my life?"

"Every part of it." Marie almost sounded proud.

"It'll never work," Elaine warned. "My friends, my family—everyone will know it's not me."

"Oh, I've already taken care of that."

"Why am I not surprised?"

"Be quiet; you might learn something. Down the hall is a memory replicator, one of my colleagues' inventions. I'll hook us both up, and your memories will be read, copied, and fed into my brain."

"I don't think so!" Elaine turned and began to run, but Marie caught up and grabbed her arms. The physicist then dragged her kicking and screaming counterpart to a small room with an ominous-looking machine. Marie strapped Elaine to a table and hooked a small helmet to her head.

"Don't do this!" Elaine shrieked, struggling against the restraints. "Please don't do this!"

Marie steadfastly ignored Elaine's protests and attached a similar helmet to her own head. She adjusted herself on the table and activated the memory replicator with a remote control. The machine whirred into life, and Elaine's violent squirming gradually subsided into subdued whimpering.

Ten minutes later the whirring slowed and eventually died. Elaine's eyes moved sluggishly as she watched Marie sit up, stretch, and smile triumphantly.

"Thank you, Elaine. I have everything I'll need in your world."

"What happens to me?" Elaine whispered, not having enough energy to talk louder.

"Oh, you'll stay here as my prisoner. I can't have you wandering loose. You don't need to worry about food; I've arranged for some to be brought here three times a day," Marie informed her.

"How long will I stay here?"

"Forever."

Elaine groaned.

ELAINE COULD NEVER remember how many days or months she stayed in her prison. Food was left for her three times a day just as Marie had said, but there was nothing with which she could occupy her attention. There were many days she was surprised she didn't die of boredom. Eating, sleeping, and exploring the building (which seemed to be an abandoned house) were the staples of her day.

One day while she was dozing, she heard footsteps treading the corridor.

Could Marie have come back? she wondered. She doubted it; these footsteps sounded heavier Maybe someone was coming to rescue her! Maybe whoever delivered her food decided to see who was receiving said food! She stood up and straightened her dress.

The man who stepped through the door stopped short when he saw her, his eyes nearly bugging out of his head. "Marie?" he gasped. "Marie, what are you doing here? I thought..."

"I'm not Marie; I'm Elaine. And who are you?" Elaine demanded.

The strange man moved closer. His face fell. "Forgive me. I thought you were Dr. Hart. She's been missing for the last four months. I'm one of her colleagues, Dr. Max Keeler, and I'm also proud to say I'm one of her friends. But your resemblance"—

"—is not coincidental," Elaine interrupted. "Dr. Keeler, how well did you know Marie?"

"It's Max, and we were as close as family. That's what makes it strange; she never told me she had a twin sister. In fact, I know she didn't have a twin sister."

Elaine remained calm despite her rapid heartbeat. Max just might be able to help her. "Does the phrase 'inter-reality jumps' mean anything to you?"

"That was one of Marie's biggest achievements!" Max burst out. He calmed down and studied Elaine more intently. "It all makes sense now. You're Marie's counterpart—and Elaine is her middle name!"

"Just as Marie is my middle name," Elaine supplied.

"So Marie disappeared and left you in her stead," Max summarized. "How did it happen?"

Elaine related what had happened. When she was finished, Max shook his head sadly. "I've known for a while Marie wasn't happy. She dropped hints here and there that she was planning a big change, but she never said what. Now I know. And you've been here the last four months?"

"Yes," Elaine nodded. "I thought for sure I'd go crazy."

"Marie, what have you done?" Max murmured.

"What are you going to do with me?" Elaine wanted to know.

"It's obvious, isn't it?" Max countered. "It's not right to keep you here. I'm going to send you back."

"Send me back!" Elaine's optimism shot through the roof. "But how?"

"By making an inter-reality jump. Marie must have the equipment stowed here somewhere. Do you have any idea where it might be?"

Elaine shook her head. "Sorry, but the only thing I know of is that memory-replicator she hooked me to before she left."

"Well, we'll just have to look for it. Come on," Max beckoned, jogging out the door. Elaine immediately followed, hardly believing that she was finally going home.

They scoured the old mansion from top to bottom without finding the mechanism for the inter-reality jumps. Max was quickly becoming more and more frustrated.

"Elaine, are you sure you haven't seen it?" Max checked.

Elaine blinked back tears, dismayed at the thought of her only hope of rescue sliding down a tunnel of oblivion. "I'm sorry, Max, but I don't even know what it looks like."

"Oh, but that's easy. It's a tall, steel device with a platform, and it comes with a remote so you can activate it from the other timeline," Max described.

"Wait, I just might know where it is."

Max grabbed her shoulders anxiously. "Where?"

"I think I found something like that when I was first exploring, but I didn't know what it was," Elaine recalled. "It was in a room not far from where I first woke up. Here, I'll show you." She grabbed Max's wrist and dragged him to probable room.

"THAT'S IT, ELAINE!" Max shouted with glee when she showed him what she had found. He dashed over to a side table and grabbed a small, silver square. "And here's the remote!"

"Why didn't Marie take it?" Elaine wondered out loud.

"She wasn't planning to come back," Max shrugged. "She didn't need it. Now let's send you home. Stand over there."

Elaine hopped onto the center platform and was surprised when Max joined her after making some adjustments to the machine. "You're coming, too?"

"Marie might need a little convincing on this," he explained. "I know she won't come willingly."

"Thanks," Elaine smiled. "So how does this work?"

"Well, if it still works, we should be transitioning right"—

The room oscillated and settled back to normal.

"—now."

Elaine looked around. "But the room hasn't changed. It didn't work."

"Are you sure?" Max questioned.

Elaine studied the room more closely. "The platform's gone!"

"We're now back in your timeline," Max told her. "Where do you think Marie would be?"

"Let me go outside and get my bearings. I still don't know where I am" She enthusiastically bolted out of the room but then paused, unsure of where the exit was.

Max joined her and gently pulled her arm. "The door is this way," he prodded.

SOON THE DUO FOUND themselves outside blinking in the bright morning sun.

"I know this place!" Elaine exclaimed, turning around to examine the house. "This house was condemned about six months ago; I remember seeing the picture in the paper. So this means we're in Huntington, and my apartment is about an hour away." Her face fell. "But that's by car, and we don't have one."

"We'll just have to ask for a ride," Max decided. "In the meantime our legs can serve us just as well."

In the end Elaine and Max had to walk the entire distance to town. Their legs were ready to drop off, but the fun hadn't really started just yet. They still had to handle Marie. As they utilized an empty park bench, they developed a plan of action.

"Where do you work?" Max asked.

"The *Daily Report* office about three blocks from here," Elaine replied. "My shift starts at nine, so Marie will be at the front desk on the first floor. I'm one of three receptionists." She blinked incredulously and pointed. "And there she is!"

Max followed the finger that pointed to a smartly dressed woman striding confidently down the sidewalk, a woman physically identical in every way to the one seated beside him. He rose and began to approach her. "I'll handle this. Wait here."

"But, Max"—Elaine began.

"I said wait!" Max snapped abruptly, breaking into a jog.

Just then Marie turned her head and noticed Max for the first time. She paled and broke into a run, but Max kept pace. They disappeared around a building.

"Max!" Elaine yelled. Nothing happened. She got up from the bench, followed the path she had seen them take, and found them standing outside a music shop conversing in hushed tones. Max placed his hand on Marie's arm, which she yanked away. Undeterred, he grabbed her arm again.

"It's over, Marie," he told her sternly.

Marie lowered her head, tears streaming down her face. "No," she whispered defiantly. Upset as she was, however, she followed Max down the sidewalk until Elaine intercepted them.

"She'll be fine," Max replied to her unspoken question. "The specialists back home will know how to treat her. It's doubtful she'll be able to return to her old job, but she should be happy at last."

Elaine glanced sadly at her counterpart before turning back to Max. "So you're going back now?"

"Yes," Max replied. "I need to get Marie back as quickly as possible, and you have a life to reclaim. Bye, Elaine."

"Bye, Max. And thank you."

Max smiled and led away Marie, leaving Elaine to reconstruct the shattered pieces of her life.

End

Quest for the Fire Blade

Author's Note: "Quest for the Fire Blade" is unique in that it actually has two endings. The original version I wrote in 2009 was much shorter, but when I submitted it to The Homeschool Literary Quarterly *in 2010, the editor asked if I would extend it. I have decided to publish both versions here. I have marked the original ending with an asterisk.*

"Hurry, Jake!" Theo called. "The sun just went down; now's the best time to look!"

"I'm coming," Jake grumbled as he rummaged for his binoculars. Theo was an amateur astronomer and felt obliged to share his hobby with his best friend. Jake often wished Theo didn't feel quite so obliged, but he couldn't really complain. Theo hated sports yet attended every single one of Jake's basketball games.

"Something might come out at any second!" Theo urged, leaning in Jake's bedroom doorway.

Jake crawled out from the vast recesses under his bed. His dark blonde hair was full of dust, but the search had yielded the long-elusive binoculars. "Theo, no one's seen any large meteors since that one in Texas in February; what makes you think you'll find another one?"

"This is America. Anything can happen," Theo shrugged.

"Whatever," Jake sighed. "Let's get this over with."

Their star-gazing positions that night were located in Jake's backyard. To be on the safe side, Theo set up his dad's camera in his backyard so it would record any stellar activities he and Jake might miss.

For two hours they stayed in the backyard. Jake began to get a crick in his neck from staring upwards for so long, but he didn't dare complain. Theo let nothing, not even neck cricks, get in the way of scientific discovery.

Finally he decided his neck couldn't withstand the agony much longer. "I don't think we'll see anything tonight. Why don't we go inside?"

Theo sighed and lowered his binoculars. "I guess you're right," he admitted, shoving his glasses back up his nose. "I wonder when there'll see another."

"Oh, it won't be for quite some time," a girl's voice remarked. "I can't go home yet."

Thoroughly startled, Jake and Theo whipped around simultaneously. Facing them was a girl completely wrapped in a black cloak with a hood thrown over her head. Her eyes lacked irises and pupils and were completely green.

"Who are you?" Jake eventually managed to stammer.

"I'm afraid you couldn't pronounce my name," the girl replied. "I am, however, interested in learning who you are."

As Theo was still in too much shock to say much of anything, Jake began speaking for them both. "Why should we tell you who we are? We don't even know who you are."

"I need some help on my mission," the girl explained. "I could force you to help me and not even bother to learn your names, but I knew the best way to work with humans would be to follow their customs."

"What mission?" Jake wanted to know.

"If you must know, I'm supposed to retrieve a weapon that was lost here long ago," the girl answered. "I landed in—what do you call it?—Texas because the weapon was last seen there, but I've been tracking it all over this continent for the last four months. I'm sure it's here, but I'm not familiar with your land masses."

"It's a pretty big country. Why do you want us to help you?" Jake repeated.

The girl gave him an odd look. "Because I've tracked the weapon to this area of the country," she informed. "My latest source indicated the weapon was hidden in a cave not far from here; do either of you know where such a cave might be?"

"Sure, everyone knows there's a big cave over on that side of town." Jake gestured

absentmindedly in what he hoped was the right direction.

It wasn't, and Theo was quick to correct him. "You pointed east, Jake. The cave sits south of here. I'm very sorry about the confusion," he apologized, turning to the girl. "Jake's terrible with directions."

"Then why don't you show me?" the girl suggested.

Jake and Theo glanced at each other.

"Why not?" Theo shrugged. He turned to the girl. "I can't speak for Jake, but I'm in."

"I guess I am, too," Jake added none too enthusiastically.

"Excellent," the girl grinned. "Follow me."

As she bounded away, Theo called after her, "What are we supposed to call you?"

She turned back and appeared to be thinking. Finally she replied, "You may call me Caitlyn. That's the closest rendering of my name I can put in your language."

"CAN'T WE REST A MINUTE?" Theo panted as they descended yet another hill. He and Jake had been following Caitlyn for about an hour, and she showed no signs of slowing down.

"But it's only three more miles," Caitlyn protested, turning confused eyes on them.

"It might as well be thirty miles," Jake grumbled as he flopped down on the grass.

Only when Caitlyn saw that the boys were determined to rest did she relent and join them on the grass. She lay on the grass and gazed thoughtfully at the night sky. Jake and Theo watched her curiously.

"Are you really from up there?" Jake eventually asked.

"What do you think?" Caitlyn countered without moving her eyes.

"But it just seems so impossible," Theo shrugged helplessly. "Lots of people here believe there are aliens; there's just been no proof. Why hasn't your race contacted Earth?"

Caitlyn propped herself up on an elbow. "We have been to Earth before. It was long before humans mastered transmitting radio waves, but I'm not exactly sure how long ago it was."

"Why did you come to Earth?" Jake wanted to know.

"We were fighting a war; in fact, the last battle happened right here on Earth. My ancestors won but accidentally lost a most valuable weapon—the Fire Blade."

She sighed and fell back on the grass. "The Fire Blade! The most glorious weapon ever forged by the hands of Tamek the Wondrous! I've never seen it, but it has lived over three thousand years in song and legend. Made of pure fire, it is considered the most lethal weapon in the galaxy and quite possibly the universe. There have been other, lesser fire blades, but there has always been one Fire Blade."

"If it was so important, how come your people have waited so long to find it?" Theo questioned.

"The war, unfortunately, didn't solve many internal problems," Caitlyn explained. "Those problems are still in existence. It was merely a coincidence that my government was able to send me to retrieve the Fire Blade." She stood up and stretched. "We've rested long enough. Let's get going."

Suppressing groans, Jake and Theo rose and followed her.

AFTER WHAT SEEMED TO the two boys an eternity, Caitlyn stood in the cave mouth, hands on her hips. She pulled a small, rectangular scanner out of a hidden pocket and held it cautiously in front of her. A small humming sound emanated from the little box.

"Are you sure this is the right cave?" she asked. "I'm not getting any readings."

"This is the only cave in town," Jake told her.

Caitlyn shrugged and continued into the cave. Jake and Theo watched her receding figure.

"Think we should help her?" Theo whispered.

"Why?" Jake wanted to know. "Her Fire Blade has nothing to do with us. Frankly, I don't care if I ever see her again." He grabbed Theo's elbow and was about to drag him away when a heart-rending wail reverberated throughout the cave.

"Caitlyn!" Theo yelled, tearing himself out of Jake's grasp and pounding down the corridor.

Jake wasn't far behind him. "Theo, get back here! Theo!" he called.

He was panting heavily by the time he reached Theo and Caitlyn. The lower half of her body was sprawled on the ground; Theo supported the upper half. Her eyes were closed and her breathing shallow.

"I found her like this," Theo related. "Should we take her to a doctor?"

"A doctor can't help her," Jake reminded his friend scornfully, kneeling by Caitlyn. "Caitlyn, can you hear me?"

Her eyes fluttered open. "It's gone," she gasped.

"What's gone?" Jake demanded.

"The Fire Blade," Caitlyn stammered. "It was here, but someone got it first! How?"

"Could someone else have been after it?" Theo suggested.

Caitlyn gasped a few more times before her breathing settled out. "No," she answered. "It was a top-secret mission; no one else knew. Unless...no, that can't be right. Can it?" She leapt up and started scouring the ground.

"What are you looking for?" Theo wanted to know.

Caitlyn didn't answer. Instead she pounced on some mysterious object in the dirt and held it triumphantly over her head. "Look at that! Exactly what I thought."

"And what did you think?" Jake asked.

"That one of my people got here first," Caitlyn revealed. "It's a boot heel made from a special material found on my planet."

"So it's no emergency," Theo summarized. She surprised them both with a grim look.

"It's more of an emergency than you might imagine. I was the only one dispatched to find the Fire Blade. The fact that someone else came here shows they left the planet for the same purpose I did but without authorization."

"What are you going to do?" Jake ventured.

Caitlyn gave him a disgusted look. "Find it, of course. And you're going to help me."

"I was afraid you might say that," Jake grumbled.

"But where are we going to look?" Theo asked.

"We aren't. My scanner is," Caitlyn replied. She pulled it out of the folds of her cloak and fiddled with the knobs. As before, the scanner hummed quietly in her hand. It beeped sporadically for a few seconds before solidifying into a strong bleeping. Caitlyn looked up and grinned.

"This way," she beckoned and took off running. Jake and Theo sighed and followed.

THE BOYS WERE GREATLY pleased when they learned that the other ship, which greatly resembled a large boulder, was parked a few feet from the cave. They crouched alongside Caitlyn as she hid behind a rock.

"What do we do now, wait for them to come out?" Jake whispered.

Caitlyn turned to look at him. "That's exactly what we do, Jake," she answered. "We can't storm their ship; it's too well fortified. Sooner or later someone will come out."

"I don't understand something, Caitlyn," Theo spoke up. "If these people have the Fire Blade, why haven't they left yet?"

"My guess is the ship is out of fuel. Earth is quite far for us," Caitlyn told him.

"If Earth is so far for you, how come you fought a battle here?" Theo pursued.

"My people were following their enemies," Caitlyn shrugged. "No distance was too great compared to potential victory. It's the way we've always been."

"Hey, I think I see someone!" Jake tugged excitedly on Caitlyn's cloak.

Theo and Caitlyn turned to see what Jake had pointed out. One shadowy figure walked in front of two others that were carrying a large chest.

"I knew it," Caitlyn breathed. "They're looking for fuel. Now's our chance." She leapt up, ran a short distance, and darted for the nearest cover. After making sure the coast was clear, she motioned for Jake and Theo to follow her. They did this with a certain amount of awkwardness.

"Are you sure this is a good idea?" Theo hesitated. "There could still be people on that ship."

"And you were the one who volunteered us for this," Jake smirked.

"This is a smuggler-type ship. It won't have more than six crewmen," Caitlyn mused. "There shouldn't be any more than three people left on board. That won't be too difficult." She glanced about one more time and dashed for the ship with Jake and Theo close behind.

A loud shout came from behind. The trio whipped around and saw one of the crewmen staring at them. Like Caitlyn he was swathed in black, and his two glowing red eyes were his only distinguishable features.

"Inside!" Caitlyn yelled, dragging Jake inside.

"Hey!" Jake yelped.

They pelted into a hallway that branched off into three directions. Without bothering to discuss, each took a different corridor. What they hadn't known (and soon learned) was that each corridor led to the same room.

A smile lit Caitlyn's face as she consulted her scanner. "It's here," she announced.

"You're sure?" Theo checked.

Before Caitlyn could answer, two men charged into the room. Instantly the girl launched herself at them.

"Come on, Jake!" Theo urged. "We have to find it."

"We don't even know what it looks like!" Jake protested.

"Just start looking," Theo snorted disgustedly.

Avoiding the wrestling bodies, the boys searched high and low for anything resembling the Fire Blade.

"Hey, Theo, I think I found something!" Jake called.

"What is it?" Theo asked as Jake pulled out what looked like a scabbard. He watched as his friend pulled slightly on the protruding handle and revealed a bright glimmer of light.

"Caitlyn, we found it!" Jake held the scabbard high above his head so she could see it.

"Make for the exit!" Caitlyn directed, still struggling with the crewmen. "I'll meet you there!"

Jake and Theo didn't question. They simply ran, hoping all the while that they wouldn't run into any angry aliens.

"We made it!" Jake gasped as they pounded outside. They halted by the rock they first hid behind and caught their breath.

"Where's Caitlyn?" Theo wondered.

"Right here," her voice sounded behind them.

Slowly the boys turned to face her. She was grinning and didn't seem to be out of breath as they were.

"I think this is yours," Jake remarked, handing her the scabbard.

"Thank you, Jake," Caitlyn smiled, accepting the Fire Blade. "Thank you, Theo. You've done me a great favor, and I doubt I'll ever be able to properly repay you." She turned and fled up the hill. Before disappearing entirely, however, she turned and waved goodbye. Then she was gone.

"Do you think we'll ever see her again?" Theo asked.

"Probably not," Jake admitted. "But I don't think we'll ever forget her."[1]

As they turned to leave, they heard an outraged, frustrated yell. Hurrying in the direction they saw Caitlyn take, they found the alien girl glaring at the scabbard as it lay on the ground.

"What's wrong, Caitlyn?" Theo questioned anxiously.

"That's not the Fire Blade," she spat through gritted teeth.

"What do you mean that's not the Fire Blade?" Jake repeated incredulously. "It's made of fire, isn't it?"

"It's of the lesser variety, ones used for ordinary weapons," Caitlyn explained, her fury subsiding yet present, nonetheless. "I have one, too. See?" She flung aside her cloak to reveal a scabbard and withdrew a fiery brand. Its flame was thinner and darker than the other sword's, but it still conveyed a thinly veiled menace.

"What's the difference?" Jake shrugged.

"You can't understand, and I don't expect you to," Caitlyn answered. "Tamek's Fire Blade was the greatest of these types of weapons; no other forger has ever come close to the mastery he accomplished. He was a true artist."

"Now what are you going to do?" Theo ventured. "Your mission's over, isn't it? At least on Earth, I mean."

As Caitlyn began to respond, three blood-chilling yells reverberated through the air. The three aliens from the ship threw themselves upon Jake, Theo, and Caitlyn. Caught off guard, the human boys defended themselves poorly, which ultimately didn't matter because Caitlyn fought valiantly enough for all three. In what seemed no time at all the leader and his companions were on their knees before Caitlyn, who held her unsheathed sword against his throat.

Jake rubbed a bruise on his arm and watched in awe as she conversed with her prisoners in their native tongue. "I never saw anyone move that fast before! Did you see what she did, Theo?"

Theo seemed considerably less enthusiastic. "Yes, I did. She's very good at this battle stuff, isn't she?"

"What's wrong?" Jake studied his friend critically.

"If the Fire Blade is half as powerful as Caitlyn says it is, maybe she shouldn't have it," Theo suggested. On seeing Jake's startled look, he continued, "We've seen her fight. If everyone on her planet is as good as she is, they must be a pretty violent bunch. Is it wise to let a people that war-happy have a weapon that strong?"

"Does it matter?" Jake countered, being careful to keep his voice low. Caitlyn seemed to be having a pretty intense conversation, and he didn't want to disturb her. "What happens on her planet doesn't concern us. We just got dragged into this whole fiasco by accident, and the sooner we get out of it, the better."

"How can you say what happens on her planet doesn't concern us!?"

"Keep your voice down; she'll hear you."

Unexpectedly Caitlyn let out an outraged shriek and launched into an unintelligible rant. The smugglers' leader responded calmly to her tirade, and she made a dismissing wave of her hand. When they had returned to their ship, she buried her head in her hands.

"Bad day at the office?" Jake queried lightly.

"He said the Fire Blade was never lost on Earth, that it was only a story invented to cover what really happened to it," she informed bleakly.

"What?" Theo burst out.

"According to him, the general who used the Fire Blade held sympathies for our enemies. He thought the war was unjust. During that last battle over Earth, he gave the Fire Blade to an enemy soldier with instructions to do with it what he saw fit."

"Are you sure the story's reliable?" Theo checked.

"The smuggler said he is descended from an aide who overheard the general's conversation with the enemy soldier, and the story has been passed down in his family for centuries. Besides, on my planet a known criminal can be killed in custody for lying, and he wanted too badly to save his own life," Caitlyn explained.

"So now that you know the Fire Blade isn't on Earth, can Theo and I go home now?" Jake wanted to know.

"Yes," Caitlyn assured him. "I thank you for your assistance; I couldn't have found the smugglers without you. Now I can really concentrate on retrieving the Fire Blade for my people."

"Before you go, Caitlyn, there's something I've been wondering," Theo spoke up.

"Ask away," Caitlyn beckoned.

"It's obvious your people know something of Earth–they know a little of our history, and it's clear you can speak our language. Do you have plans of–um–invading Earth?"

"Not at the moment," she answered. "We don't see any benefits our empire would receive from Earth, so you're safe."

Theo sighed in relief and grinned at Jake.

"However, if humans make significant progress in any direction, and the government decides we would benefit from Earth's research, we'll be back," Caitlyn added.

Jake and Theo froze in horror.

"I'll be leaving now. Thank you again for your help." She smiled and ran off.

"Caitlyn, wait!" Theo shouted. He dashed after her and grabbed the edge of her cloak to slow her down. She turned and glared at him.

"Theo, you idiot! Wait for me!" Jake yelled, his legs pelting to catch up with Caitlyn and Theo as they engaged in a fierce tug-of-war over the cloth.

"Let go!" Caitlyn ordered.

"No! Help, Jake!"

Jake caught up to Theo and assisted in yanking Caitlyn to the ground. Before she had the chance to get back up, Jake grabbed her arms and held them behind her back. Caitlyn kicked him in the shins, threw him to the ground, and scrambled to her feet. She unsheathed her sword and leveled it at the boys.

"Do not try to hinder me," she warned. "I may be young in your eyes, but among my people I am a candidate for a high-ranking military position. That is why the government sent me, to determine my aptitude for battle and ability to improvise in alien cultures. Only the best commanders lead the army into battle."

"We don't care about your stupid army!" Theo spat. "We just want our planet to be safe."

"I've already told you your planet is safe," she reminded, "as long as there are no major advancements."

"How do we know we can trust you?" Theo persisted.

"My people would never invade and conquer a planet unless they deemed it worth their time," Caitlyn explained.

"I think Theo wants a promise that you'll never invade Earth," Jake hinted.

"I don't have that authority!" Caitlyn protested. "I am a princess of the royal family, true, but I was not sent on a diplomatic mission. I don't have the necessary qualifications that would make such a promise binding on my government."

Jake and Theo glanced at each other.

"If it helps, I can argue that Earth does not show promise of any significant developments and propose we classify it as inconsequential," Caitlyn suggested. "We'd ignore Earth in all our dealings, so you'd be perfectly safe."

Theo paused to consider her offer. "All right," he agreed. "It seems fair, after all. We helped you with your mission even if the Fire Blade wasn't here."

"I do appreciate everything you've done to help me," Caitlyn reiterated. "I only needed someone to help me, but I must admit I've grown fond of you in your own human way."

"Thanks," Jake responded sarcastically as Theo helped him up.

"Well, goodbye again." Caitlyn waved her hand and left the boys.

"What do you think of that, Jake? We saved the world tonight," Theo commented proudly.

"Yeah, I guess we did."

"Do you still think astronomy is dumb?"

"Yes."

"Well, I guess you can't win them all."

End

[1] Original 2009 ending